W9-AAT-644

E TUPPER LING

Tupper Ling, Nancy

The story I'll tell

HUDSON PUBLIC LIBRARY
3 WASHINGTON STREET
@ WOOD SQUARE
HUDSON, MA 01749

HUDSON
PUBLIC LIBRARY

WITHDRAWN
FROM OUR
COLLECTION

The Story I'll Tell

NOV 21 2015

HUDSON PUBLIC LIBRARY
WOOD SQUARE
HUDSON, MA 01749

Text copyright © 2015 by Nancy Tupper Ling • Illustrations copyright © 2015 by Jessica Lanan
All rights reserved. No part of this book may be reproduced, transmitted, or stored in an information
retrieval system in any form or by any means, electronic, mechanical, photocopying, recording, or otherwise,
without written permission from the publisher.
LEE & LOW BOOKS Inc., 95 Madison Avenue, New York, NY 10016, leeandlow.com
Book design by Stephanie Bart-Horvath • Book production by The Kids at Our House
The text is set in Adobe Jenson Pro • The illustrations are rendered in watercolor and colored pencil.
Manufactured in China by Nordica International Ltd., August 2015
10 9 8 7 6 5 4 3 2 1
First Edition
Library of Congress Cataloging-in-Publication Data
Tupper Ling, Nancy.
The story I'll tell / by Nancy Tupper Ling ; illustrations by Jessica Lanan.
— First edition.   pages cm
Summary: "A mother weaves a magical web of tales to explain how her child came to be a part
of the family" — Provided by publisher.
ISBN 978-1-62014-160-1 (hardcover : alk. paper)
[1. Intercountry adoption — Fiction. 2. Adoption — Fiction. 3. Mother and child — Fiction.]
I. Lanan, Jessica, illustrator. II. Title. III. Title: Story I will tell.
PZ7.1.T873St 2015   [E]—dc23   2015009655

FSC
www.fsc.org
MIX
Paper from
responsible sources
FSC® C112492

The Story I'll Tell

by Nancy Tupper Ling

illustrations by Jessica Lanan

LEE & LOW BOOKS INC.   NEW YORK

To the adoptive families who have inspired me
Soli Deo Gloria —N.T.L.

To my grandfather, who loved beautiful books —J.L.

Someday when you ask where you came from,
I'll tell you a story.

I might tell how you came from a land far away in a hot-air balloon. The basket slowly drifted down like a feather into our yard. I dropped the firewood I was carrying and ran to you.

"You're home now," I said. Then I wrapped you in a blanket as red and silky as the balloon's sails.

Or maybe the blanket was silver, and it belonged to
the silent horseman who rode into our valley. He carried
you on his stallion the way the postman brings the mail.

I saw you tucked inside his satchel, your wisps of dark
hair blowing in the breeze. You didn't cry as he placed
you in my arms.

"No, not a horseman," I'll say.
"An angel. That's who brought you."
Wrapped in her arms, you followed a
trail of lanterns around the world until you
reached our doorstep.
I'll always wonder how she picked our home.
We don't have fancy gates or marble stairs,
but she found the perfect place for you.
How your eyes sparkled when I first saw you.

Or was it a lark that announced your arrival.
I opened the door to its song high in our birch tree.
When I climbed to the top, you were cradled in the
branches. Did you know I'd never let you fall? Your
hands fluttered like leaves when the clouds passed by.

When I was a child, Grandma said I came from a patch of cabbages in her garden. I guess I could use that story too. But I'd say we found you under the tiger lilies. Their pollen fell onto your cheeks like freckles.

Perhaps we were walking on the beach at night,
and you floated in on a wave.

No, not a wave! I'd say there was a dragon queen
who kept you by the sea to raise you as her own.
I heard cooing sounds calling to me.

I waited until the dragon queen fell asleep. Then I
tiptoed inside and rescued you from her dark cave.

"Not true!" you'll say when I tell these tales.
And I'll smile, because it will be hard to fool the
brightest child in the world.

Still, there are times when I think I will tell you the truth, for the truth is a beautiful story too.

And so when you ask where you came from, I will tell you how we gathered you in a silk blanket and flew on wings through the sky. Your eyes sparkled like the ocean below, and your hands fluttered as clouds passed by.

And when I looked into your tiny face, it was your eyebrows that I noticed right away. Oh, those eyebrows! They told the story of a distant land. They rose up like the mountains of Yunnan.

Or maybe you came into town with the August moon.
Lion dancers pranced around you. Musicians plucked
their fiddles. I climbed onto the float and I held you
tight, our two worlds meeting there on Main Street.
Your smile was as wide as the ocean when I cradled you.

When we brought you home in dawn's early light, you
cried for things lost and new. I smoothed down your
sweet hair and hummed the first of many songs to come.

That's when you smiled, a smile as warm as the
sun. And I knew then. You were the best gift we had
ever received.